Be Careful, Banjo!

An Ivy and Mack Story

Written by Juliet Clare Bell

Illustrated by Gustavo Mazali

with Dusan Pavlic

Collins

Download the audio at www.collins.co.uk/839811

woods
birds
squirrel

Ivy and Mack are happy. Today they can see Grandpa!

“I want to make a cake with Grandpa!” said Ivy. “I’ve got some strawberries to put on the top! Look!”

“Can I eat one?” asked Mack.

“No!” said Ivy. “Grandpa loves strawberries. They’re for the cake!”

Ivy ran into Grandpa's house. "Let's make a cake, Grandpa!" she said.

"Wait, Ivy!" said Grandpa. "Banjo needs his walk."

"Oh good!" said Mack. "Can we go to the woods? We can climb trees."

“What a good idea!” said Dad.
“The woods are great in autumn.”

“I don’t want to go for a walk,” said Ivy.

“Ivy, you love climbing trees with Mack
and you love counting the birds
with Grandpa!” said Dad.

“No, I don’t,” said Ivy. “I love
making cakes.”

"But, Ivy," said Mack, "you love Banjo, too. He wants a walk."

"*Urggh!* OK," said Ivy.

"You can't ride a skateboard in the woods," said Mack.

"Yes, I can!" said Ivy. "There's a path!"

“Climb this tree with me, Ivy,” said Mack.

“I can’t,” said Ivy. “I’m on my skateboard.”

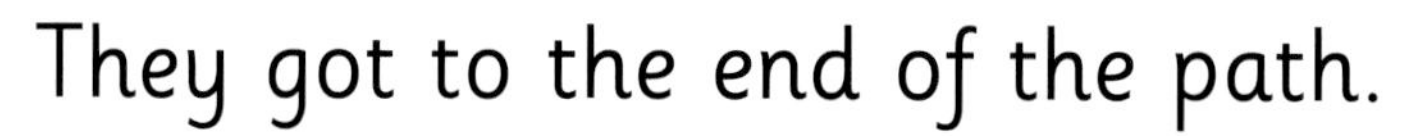

They got to the end of the path.

“I can’t use my skateboard now!” said Ivy.

“Count the birds with me, Ivy,”
said Grandpa.

“Look at the wind in the trees, Ivy!” said Mack. “It’s great!”

“My hair!” said Ivy.

"Banjo's jumping in puddles. Let's jump with him, Ivy!" said Mack.

The water from the puddle went on Ivy and on her skateboard.

Grandpa walked up to Ivy. “What’s wrong?” he said. “You always like walks with me and Banjo.”

“I’m sorry,” said Ivy. “But I’m wet now. And look at the strawberries!”

“Strawberries?” said Grandpa.

“They’re for the top of the cake!” said Ivy.

“*What* cake?” asked Grandpa.

Then Banjo saw a squirrel.

“Be careful, Banjo …” said Grandpa.

Ow!

Ivy helped Grandpa to stand up.

"Are you OK?" asked Mack.

"Can you walk?" asked Ivy.

"Don't worry," said Grandpa. "I'm OK, but it's difficult to walk."

Ivy took Grandpa's phone from his bag.

"I'm calling Mum," she said. "Oh no! It's not working."

"What do we do, Ivy?" asked Mack.

"I know! My friend Mina lives next to this forest. Can you walk to her house, Grandpa?"

"I can try," said Grandpa.

Mack gave Grandpa a big stick.

"I'm sorry I was angry," said Ivy. "I counted the birds. I saw 14."

"15 now!" said Grandpa.

Mina's grandma opened the door.

"Grandpa hurt his foot!" said Ivy.

"Come in!" said Mina's grandma.
"Mina! Quick! Get the peas!"

"*Peas?*" said Mack.

“Mum! Grandpa’s got peas on his foot!” said Mack.

“Good idea. Thank you,” said Mum to Mina’s grandma. “I can take you home now, Dad,” she said to Grandpa.

“Ivy, Mack and Banjo can stay here with us,” said Mina’s grandma.

"What would you like to do?" asked Mina's grandma.

Ivy smiled. "Can we make a cake for Grandpa? I've got strawberries for the top!"

But silly Banjo wanted to play.

"Be careful, Banjo!" said Ivy.

Picture dictionary

Listen and repeat 

climb

puddle

skateboard

squirrel

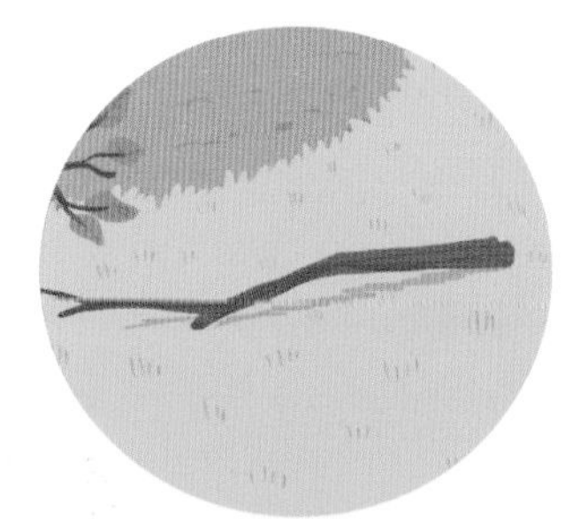

stick

strawberries

wind

woods

1 Look and order the story

2 Listen and say  

Collins

Published by Collins
An imprint of HarperCollins*Publishers*
Westerhill Road
Bishopbriggs
Glasgow
G64 2QT

HarperCollins*Publishers*
1st Floor, Watermarque Building
Ringsend Road
Dublin 4
Ireland

William Collins' dream of knowledge for all began with the publication of his first book in 1819.

A self-educated mill worker, he not only enriched millions of lives, but also founded a flourishing publishing house. Today, staying true to this spirit, Collins books are packed with inspiration, innovation and practical expertise. They place you at the centre of a world of possibility and give you exactly what you need to explore it.

10 9 8 7 6 5 4 3 2

ISBN 978-0-00-839811-8

www.collins.co.uk/elt

British Library Cataloguing in Publication Data

A catalogue record for this publication is available from the British Library.

Author: Juliet Clare Bell
Lead illustrator: Gustavo Mazali (Beehive)
Copy illustrator: Dusan Pavlic (Beehive)
Series editor: Rebecca Adlard
Publishing manager: Lisa Todd
Product managers: Jennifer Hall and Caroline Green
In-house editor: Alma Puts Keren
Project manager: Emily Hooton
Editor: Deborah Friedland
Proofreaders: Natalie Murray and Michael Lamb
Cover designer: Kevin Robbins
Typesetter: 2Hoots Publishing Services Ltd
Audio produced by id audio, London
Reading guide author: Julie Penn
Production controller: Rachel Weaver
Printed and bound by: GPS Group, Slovenia

MIX
Paper from responsible sources
FSC™ C007454

This book is produced from independently certified FSC™ paper to ensure responsible forest management.

For more information visit: **www.harpercollins.co.uk/green**

Download the audio for this book and a reading guide for parents and teachers at www.collins.co.uk/839811